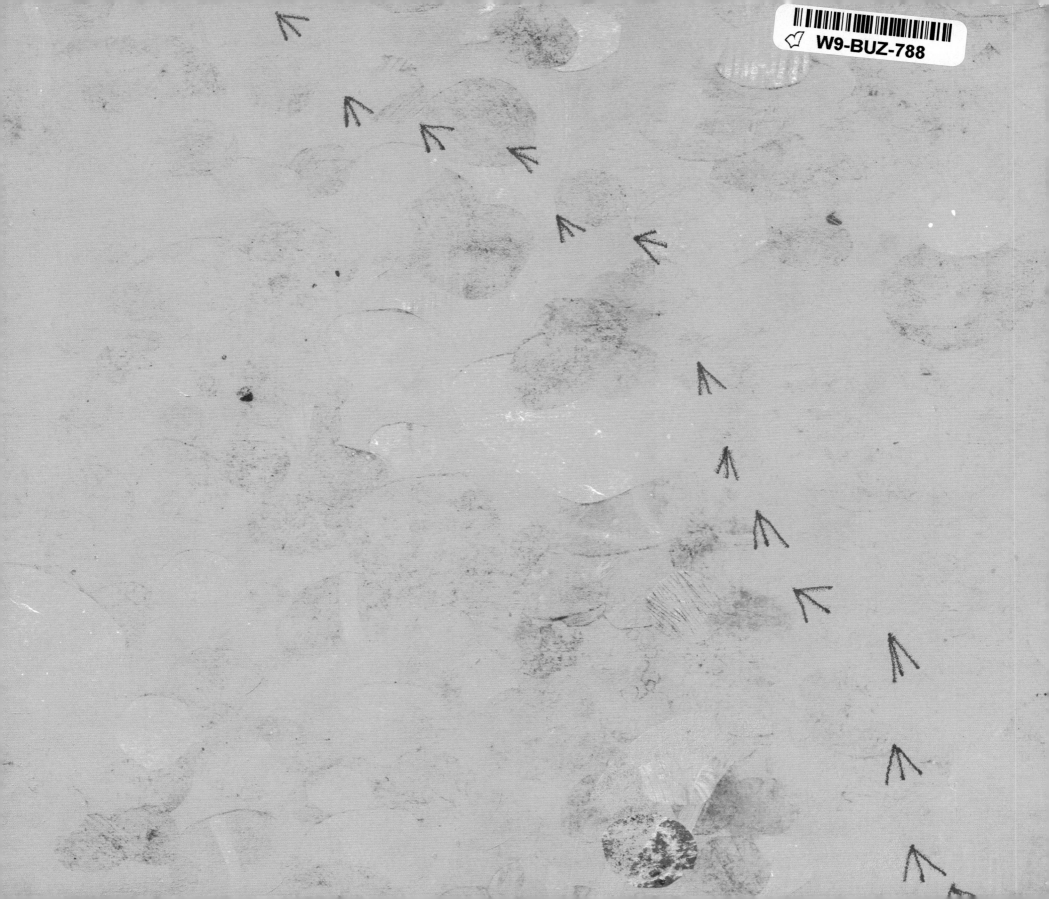

The Real Boat

MARINA AROMSHTAM

ILLUSTRATED BY

VICTORIA SEMYKINA

TRANSLATED FROM RUSSIAN BY OLGA VARSHAVER

templar books
an imprint of Candlewick Press

A paper boat was sailing in a pond.
The pond seemed very big and deep to the little boat.
When the breeze blew, ripples ran across the surface
and rocked him.

He felt very happy.

Two googly-eyed frogs were sitting on the bank.

"Croak! Croak-croak?" asked one.
"Croak-croakity-croak," answered the other.

In frog language this meant:

"Look! What's that? Where did that come from?"

"Humans are always throwing trash in the water."

But the paper boat could speak frog language.

"I'm not trash! I'm a boat!" he said.

"A boat?" the frogs asked. "Croak! What's a boat?"

A duck landed in the water. "What's going on here?" she asked.

"Croak! That thing there claims that he's a boat."

"Quack!" said the duck. She thought for a minute, then said "quack" again. "Once, a long time ago, I flew to the tropics."

"And why should we care?" replied the frogs.

"When I was flying," said the duck, "I saw real boats. Sailing on the ocean."

"What's an ocean?" asked the paper boat.

"Quack! The ocean has lots and lots of water."

"Even more than we have here?" asked the frogs in amazement.

"Quack! The ocean has so much water that it joins the sky."

I want to sail on the ocean, too, just like a real boat!
thought the paper boat.

Croak

A stream trickled out of the pond, and the paper boat
sailed along it. The frogs followed him.

"Croak-croak! We're going to the ocean, too."

But before long, the frogs got tired, and the paper boat sailed on alone.

The stream got wider and wider.

"Wow! There's so much water!" marveled the paper boat.
"This must be the way to the ocean!"
There was a rowboat near the riverbank, and the paper boat
bobbed alongside.

"Shhh! Don't be so noisy!" grumbled the old rowboat.
You'll scare away all the fish!"

"Could you be so kind as to tell me where the ocean is?"
said the paper boat, trying to whisper.

"Ocean? Never heard of it. Go away! I won't catch any fish
with you shouting like that."

What a grump! thought the paper boat,
and he went on his way.

After a while, the stream joined another stream and became a river.
The banks were even farther away now. A motorboat roared past.

"Tell me, please, how can I get to the ocean?" the paper boat called out.
But the motorboat was already gone.

Soon, a riverboat came around the bend. The paper boat thought it was lovely—how delightful it would be to sail along with music playing!

But the riverboat didn't know the way to the ocean.
"I just take passengers up and down the river.
Try asking the barge over there."

In the distance was a barge piled
high with sand.

When the barge got closer, the paper boat said,
"You must be really strong to carry so much sand!"

"I can carry gravel, too," said the barge proudly,
"and sometimes even coal!"

The paper boat suddenly realized that the barge wasn't moving by herself—
a small, sturdy boat was pushing her from behind, huffing and puffing.

"Now *you* really are a strong boat!" said the paper boat with admiration.

"I'm a tugboat. I chug along all right, but I can't go very fast," answered the tugboat.

"Do you know how to get to the ocean?"

"I'm taking this barge to the port. You can come if you like. Someone there will know."

The paper boat pulled alongside the tugboat and tried to huff and puff just like him.

The river grew wider and wider, and fancy yachts and
sailboats glided up and down.

Finally, the tops of tall cranes appeared in the distance, and then—ships! Lots and lots of ships! Passenger liners, container ships, fishing trawlers, cargo ships. White seagulls flew overhead. It was a breathtaking sight!

"Soon we'll be in the harbor," explained the tugboat. "Go and find someone who knows the way to the ocean. Chug-a-chug! Toot, toot!"

There was so much to see in the harbor!

Ships were loaded and unloaded. Tall cranes raised
and lowered shipping containers.

In one cage were two giraffes. A crane picked the cage up as
though it was empty and carefully set it down on the dock.

At the wharf, one end of a ferry boat swung open and formed a ramp. A car drove out, then another, and another, and another.

The paper boat counted the cars up to a hundred (which was as high as he could count), and still they kept coming.

Soon it was dark, and lights came on all over the port.
A passenger liner shone like an enchanted city.

"Do you know the way to the ocean?" asked the paper boat.

"I'm going there first thing tomorrow," the ship replied.

But when the paper boat woke up the next morning, the passenger liner was already leaving the harbor.

"You wouldn't be going to the ocean, would you?" the paper boat asked a fishing trawler.

"Of course I am!"

"Can I follow you?"

"Come along! But be careful not to get caught up in my net!" the trawler said with a laugh.

And the paper boat sailed behind him.

Then the paper boat saw something
strange and frightening. Smoke-
stacks rose from the water
like parts of a sea monster's body.

"That's a loading dock for tankers,"
the trawler said. "And that is my
old friend Supertanker. See that big
pump filling him full of oil?"

Tied up next to the loading dock
was a ship as big as an island.

"Hey there, Floating Tin Can!" the fishing trawler called out to the tanker.

"Hi, Fish Catcher," replied the tanker. "I could smell you coming a mile away."

"You should talk! Do you think you smell like roses? They won't even let you into the port! You have to sit out here by yourself."

"Yes, it is kind of lonely," agreed the tanker.

"Well, you take good care of your belly. You don't want any oil to spill into the sea. See you later! The fish will be wondering where I am!"

"Goodbye for now," said the tanker.

The port grew smaller and smaller in the distance until they couldn't even see ships anymore. And there was no land in sight—just water and more water, stretching to the sky.

The paper boat was sailing on the ocean, on the real ocean! He bounced on the waves and splashed. He even tried to whistle like an ocean liner, but he could only make a funny little beep.

After a while, dark clouds appeared on the horizon. They moved across the sky like sharks, swallowing everything in their path. First they swallowed up the fluffy white clouds, then the sun, and finally the last slice of blue sky.

Blinding bolts of lightning flashed, and there were deafening roars of thunder. The water turned black—as black as the sky—and the waves grew bigger.

The paper boat was tossed high and then came crashing down.
"Where are you?" called the trawler. "Try to stay close to me!"

Just then, a huge wave caught the paper boat and carried him far away.

When the storm had passed, the trawler was nowhere
to be seen. The sea grew calm and sunlight danced on the
still water. The paper boat was very frightened. The storm had
battered him badly, and he was all alone on the huge ocean.

Just then, an unknown ship came out of the fog like a ghost.
It had antennas and radar transmitters sticking out
everywhere.

It was one of the naval fleet's destroyers. The destroyer seemed cold and expressionless, and the paper boat didn't dare speak to him.

Then the destroyer disappeared back into the fog, as though he had never been there at all.

The paper boat had completely filled with water, and he started to sink. As he sank deeper into the ocean, there was less and less light, and the water pressed down on him more and more.

Finally he reached the ocean floor. He sighed sadly. "Will I spend the rest of time down here among the fish?"

But just then something strange was heading toward him with a bright spotlight.

"Did you sink, too?" asked the paper boat.
"Are we partners in misfortune?"

"We're not partners of any sort! I am a submarine.
I sink down whenever I want. And then when
I want to, I go back up," replied the submarine,
and she rose toward the surface.

The paper boat was left alone again.

But then came a man in a diving suit!

Here is a paper boat! Would you believe it? thought the diver.

The diver climbed back on board the research ship
and handed the paper boat to his captain.

"How in the world did you wind up at the bottom of the ocean?"
the captain asked. "You're so tiny—you must have sailed so far!

A true seafarer!

A real boat!"

"A real boat needs a name," the captain said.

He cut a plaque out of cardboard and wrote on it in fancy letters:

INTREPID

Then he glued the plaque onto the side of the paper boat.

The paper boat sighed happily.

At last, he was a real boat.

For my grandsons Sam and Gorge,
whom I wish to become real boats
M. A.

First U.S. edition 2019

Library of Congress Catalog Card Number pending
ISBN 978-1-5362-0277-9

18 19 20 21 22 23 TWP 10 9 8 7 6 5 4 3 2 1

Printed in Johor Bahru, Malaysia

This book was typeset in Century Schoolbook.
The illustrations were done in mixed media.

TEMPLAR BOOKS
an imprint of
Candlewick Press
99 Dover Street
Somerville, Massachusetts 02144

www.candlewick.com

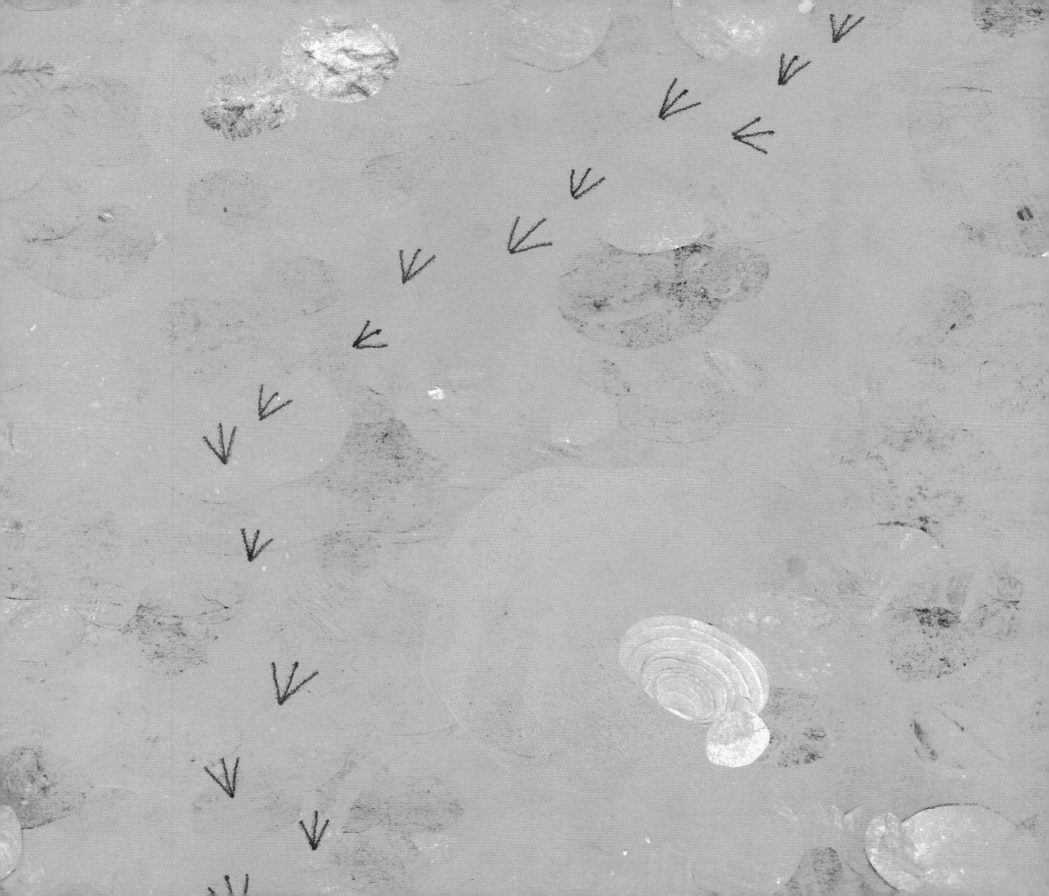